KU-594-478

HORRID HENRY
AND THE
SECRET CLUB

Francesca Simon

Illustrated by Tony Ross

Orion
Children's Books

For Susan Winter, without whom . . .

Published in paperback in 1996
First published in Great Britain in 1995
by Orion Children's Books
a division of the Orion Publishing Group Ltd
Orion House
5 Upper St Martin's Lane
London WC2H 9EA

An Hachette Livre UK Company

This edition published in 2000

6

Text Copyright © Francesca Simon 1995
Illustrations Copyright © Tony Ross 1995

The right of Francesca Simon and Tony Ross
to be identified as author and illustrator
of this work has been asserted.

All rights reserved. No part of this publication may
be reproduced, stored in a retrieval system, or transmitted,
in any form or by any means, electronic, mechanical,
photocopying, recording or otherwise, without the
prior permission of Orion Children's Books.

The Orion Publishing Group's policy is to use papers that
are natural, renewable and recyclable products and
made from wood grown in sustainable forests. The logging
and manufacturing processes are expected to conform to
the environmental regulations of the country of origin.

A catalogue record for this book
is available from the British Library

Typeset by Deltatype Ltd, Birkenhead
Printed in Great Britain by Clays Ltd, St Ives plc

www.orionbooks.co.uk

HORRID HENRY

AND THE
SECRET CLUB

Francesca Simon is an American who lives
in London with her English husband and
her son. She grew up in California, was
educated at Yale and Oxford Universities,
and was a freelance journalist, writing theatre
and restaurant reviews for some years. She
is now a very successful writer of children's
books, ranging from picture books to young
fiction.

Also by Francesca Simon

Horrid Henry
Horrid Henry Tricks the Tooth Fairy
Horrid Henry's Nits
Horrid Henry Gets Rich Quick
Horrid Henry's Haunted House
Horrid Henry and the Mummy's Curse
Horrid Henry's Revenge
Horrid Henry and the Bogey Babysitter
Horrid Henry's Stinkbomb
Horrid Henry's Underpants
Horrid Henry Meets the Queen
Horrid Henry and the Mega-Mean Time Machine
Horrid Henry and the Football Fiend
Horrid Henry's Christmas Cracker

Horrid Henry's Big Bad Book
Horrid Henry's Wicked Ways
Horrid Henry's Evil Enemies
Horrid Henry's Joke Book

Don't Cook Cinderella
Helping Hercules

and for younger readers
Don't Be Horrid, Henry
Illustrated by Kevin McAleenan
The Topsy-Turvies
Illustrated by Emily Bolam

CONTENTS

1

HORRID HENRY'S INJECTION

"AAGGHH!!"

"AAAGGGGHHH!!!!"

"AAAAAGGGGGHHHHH !!!!"

The horrible screams came from behind Nurse Needle's closed door.

Horrid Henry looked at his younger brother Perfect Peter. Perfect Peter looked at Horrid Henry. Then they both looked at their father, who stared straight ahead.

Henry and Peter were in Dr Dettol's waiting room.

Moody Margaret was there. So were Sour Susan, Anxious Andrew, Jolly Josh, Weepy William, Tough Toby, Lazy Linda, Clever Clare, Rude Ralph and just about everyone Henry knew. They were all waiting for the terrible moment when Nurse Needle would call their name.

Today was the worst day in the world. Today was – injection day.

Horrid Henry was not afraid of spiders.

He was not afraid of spooks.

He was not afraid of burglars, bad dreams, squeaky doors and things that go bump in the night. Only one thing scared him.

Just thinking about . . . about . . . Henry could barely even say the word – INJECTIONS – made him shiver and quiver and shake and quake.

Nurse Needle came into the
waiting room.

Henry held his breath.

"Please let it be someone else," he
prayed.

"William!" said Nurse Needle.

Weepy William burst into tears.

"Let's have none of that," said
Nurse Needle. She took him firmly
by the arm and closed the door
behind him.

"I don't need an injection!" said Henry. "I feel fine."

"Injections stop you getting ill," said Dad. "Injections fight germs."

"I don't believe in germs," said Henry.

"I do," said Dad.

"I do," said Peter.

"Well, I don't," said Henry.

Dad sighed. "You're having an injection, and that's that."

"I don't mind injections," said Perfect Peter. "I know how good they are for me."

Horrid Henry pretended he was an alien who'd come from outer space to jab earthlings.

'OWW!' shrieked Peter.

'Don't be horrid, Henry!' shouted Dad.

"AAAAAAGGGGGHHHHHH!"

came the terrible screams from behind Nurse Needle's door.

"AAAAAAGGGGGHHHHH! NOOOOOOOO!"

Then Weepy William staggered out, clutching his arm and wailing.

"Crybaby," said Henry.

"Just wait, Henry," sobbed William.

Nurse Needle came into the waiting room.

Henry closed his eyes.

"Don't pick me," he begged silently. "Don't pick me."

"Susan!" said Nurse Needle.

Sour Susan crept into Nurse Needle's office.

"AAAAAAGGGGGHHHHHH!" came the terrible screams.

"AAAAAAGGGGGHHHHH! NOOOOOOO!"

Then Sour Susan dragged herself out, clutching her arm and snivelling.

"What a crybaby," said Henry.

"Well, we all know about *you*, Henry," said Susan sourly.

"Oh yeah?" said Henry. "You don't know anything."

Nurse Needle reappeared.

Henry hid his face behind his hands.

I'll be so good if it's not me, he thought. Please, let it be someone else.

"Margaret!" said Nurse Needle.

Henry relaxed.

"Hey, Margaret, did you know the needles are so big and sharp they can go right through your arm?' said Henry.

Moody Margaret ignored him and marched into Nurse Needle's office.

Henry could hardly wait for her terrible screams. Boy, would he tease that crybaby Margaret!

Silence.

Then Moody Margaret swaggered into the waiting room, proudly displaying an enormous plaster on her arm. She smiled at Henry.

"Ooh, Henry, you won't believe the needle she's using today," said Margaret. "It's as long as my leg."

"Shut up, Margaret," said Henry. He was breathing very fast and felt faint.

"Anything wrong, Henry?' asked Margaret sweetly.

"No," said Henry. He scowled at her. How dare she not scream and cry?

"Oh, good," said Margaret. "I just wanted to warn you because I've never seen such big fat whopping needles in all my life!"

Horrid Henry steadied himself. Today would be different.

He would be brave.

He would be fearless.

He would march into Nurse Needle's office, offer his arm, and dare her to do her worst. Yes, today was the day. Brave Henry, he would be called, the boy who laughed when the needle went in, the boy who asked for a second injection, the boy who –

"Henry!" said Nurse Needle.

"NO!" shrieked Henry. "Please, please, NO!"

"Yes," said Nurse Needle. "It's your turn now."

Henry forgot he was brave.

Henry forgot he was fearless.

Henry forgot everyone was watching him.

Henry started screaming and screeching and kicking.

"OW!" yelped Dad.

"OW!" yelped Perfect Peter.

"OW!" yelped Lazy Linda.

Then everyone started screaming and screeching.

"I don't want an injection!" shrieked Horrid Henry.

"I don't want an injection!" shrieked Anxious Andrew.

"I don't want an injection!" shrieked Tough Toby.

"Stop it," said Nurse Needle. "You need an injection and an injection is what you will get."

"Him first!" screamed Henry, pointing at Peter.

"You're such a baby, Henry," said Clever Clare.

That did it.

No one *ever* called Henry a baby and lived.

He kicked Clare as hard as he could. Clare screamed.

Nurse Needle and Dad each grabbed one of Henry's arms and dragged him howling into her office. Peter followed behind, whistling softly.

Henry wriggled free and dashed out. Dad nabbed him and brought him back. Nurse Needle's door clanged shut behind them.

Henry stood in the corner. He was trapped.

Nurse Needle kept her distance. Nurse Needle knew Henry. Last time he'd had an injection he'd kicked her.

Dr Dettol came in.

"What's the trouble, Nurse?" she asked.

"Him," said Nurse Needle. "He doesn't want an injection."

18

Dr Dettol kept her distance. Dr Dettol knew Henry. Last time he'd had an injection he'd bitten her.

"Take a seat, Henry," said Dr Dettol.

Henry collapsed in a chair. There was no escape.

"What a fuss over a little thing like an injection," said Dr Dettol. "Call me if you need me," she added, and left the room.

Henry sat on the chair, breathing hard. He tried not to look as Nurse Needle examined her gigantic pile of syringes.

But he could not stop himself peeking through his fingers. He watched as she got the injection ready, choosing the longest, sharpest, most wicked needle Henry had ever seen.

Then Nurse Needle approached, weapon in hand.

"Him first!" shrieked Henry.

Perfect Peter sat down and rolled up his sleeve.

"I'll go first," said Peter. "I don't mind."

"Oh," he said, as he was jabbed.

"That was perfect," said Nurse Needle.

"What a good boy you are," said Dad.

Perfect Peter smiled proudly.

Nurse Needle rearmed herself.

Horrid Henry shrank back in the chair. He looked around wildly,

Then Henry noticed the row of little medicine bottles lined up on the counter. Nurse Needle was filling her injections from them.

Henry looked closer. The labels

read: "Do NOT give injection if a child is feverish or seems ill."

Nurse Needle came closer, brandishing the injection. Henry coughed.

And closer. Henry sneezed.

And closer. Henry wheezed and rasped and panted.

Nurse Needle lowered her arm.

"Are you all right, Henry?"

"No," gasped Henry. "I'm ill. My chest hurts, my head hurts, my throat hurts."

Nurse Needle felt his sweaty forehead.

Henry coughed again, a dreadful throaty cough.

"I can't breathe," he choked. "Asthma."

"You don't have asthma, Henry," said Dad.

"I do, too," said Henry, gasping for breath.

Nurse Needle frowned.

"He is a little warm," she said.

"I'm ill," whispered Henry pathetically. "I feel terrible."

Nurse Needle put down her syringe.

"I think you'd better bring him back when he's feeling better," she said.

"All right," said Dad. He'd make sure Henry's mother brought him next time.

Henry wheezed and sneezed, moaned and groaned, all the way home. His parents put him straight to bed.

"Oh, Mum," said Henry, trying to sound as weak as possible. "Could you bring me some chocolate ice cream to soothe my throat? It really hurts."

"Of course,' said Mum. "You poor boy."

Henry snuggled down in the cool sheets. Ahh, this was the life.

"Oh, Mum," added Henry, coughing. "Could you bring up the

23

TV? Just in case my head stops hurting long enough for me to watch?"

"Of course," said Mum.

Boy, this was great! thought Henry.

No injection! No school tomorrow!
Supper in bed!

There was a knock on the door. It
must be Mum with his ice cream.
Henry sat up in bed, then
remembered he was ill. He lay back
and closed his eyes.

"Come in, Mum," said Henry
hoarsely.

"Hello Henry."

Henry opened his eyes. It wasn't
Mum. It was Dr Dettol.

Henry closed his eyes and had a
terrible coughing fit.

"What hurts?" said Dr Dettol.

"Everything," said Henry. "My
head, my throat, my chest, my eyes,
my ears, my back and my legs."

"Oh dear," said Dr Dettol.

She took out her stethoscope and
listened to Henry's chest. All clear.

She stuck a little stick in his mouth and told him to say "AAAAAH." All clear.

She examined his eyes and ears, his back and his legs. Everything seemed fine.

"Well, Doctor?" said Mum.

Dr Dettol shook her head. She looked grave.

"He's very ill," said Dr Dettol. "There's only one cure."

"What?" said Mum.

"What?" said Dad.

"An injection!"

2

HORRID HENRY
AND THE
SECRET CLUB

"Halt! Who goes there?"

"Me."

"Who's me?" said Moody
Margaret.

"ME!" said Sour Susan.

"What's the password?"

"Uhhhh . . ." Sour Susan paused.
What was the password? She thought
and thought and thought.

"Potatoes?"

Margaret sighed loudly. Why was

she friends with such a stupid person?

"No it isn't."

"Yes it is," said Susan.

"Potatoes was last week's password," said Margaret.

"No it wasn't."

"Yes it was," said Moody Margaret. "It's my club and I decide."

There was a long pause.

"All right," said Susan sourly. "What *is* the password?"

"I don't know if I'm going to tell you," said Margaret. "I could be giving away a big secret to the enemy."

"But I'm not the enemy," said Susan. "I'm Susan."

"Shhhh!" said Margaret. "We don't want Henry to find out who's in the secret club."

Susan looked quickly over her shoulder. The enemy was nowhere to be seen. She whistled twice.

"All clear," said Sour Susan. "Now let me in."

Moody Margaret thought for a moment. Letting someone in without the password broke the first club rule.

"Prove to me you're Susan, and not the enemy pretending to be Susan," said Margaret.

"You know it's me," wailed Susan.

"Prove it."

Susan stuck her foot into the tent.

"I'm wearing the black patent leather shoes with the blue flowers I always wear."

"No good," said Margaret. "The enemy could have stolen them."

"I'm speaking with Susan's voice and I look like Susan," said Susan.

"No good," said Margaret. "The enemy could be a master of disguise."

Susan stamped her foot. "And I know that you were the one who pinched Helen and I'm going to tell Miss . . ."

"Come closer to the tent flap," said Margaret.

Susan bent over.

"Now listen to me," said Margaret. "Because I'm only going to tell you once. When a secret club member wants to come in they say 'NUNGA.' Anyone inside answers back, 'Nunga Nu.' That's how I know it's you and you know it's me."

"Nunga," said Sour Susan.

"Nunga Nu," said Moody Margaret. "Enter."

Susan entered the club. She gave

the secret handshake, sat down on her box and sulked.

"You knew it was me all along," said Susan.

Margaret scowled at her.

"That's not the point. If you don't want to obey the club rules you can leave."

Susan didn't move.

"Can I have a biscuit?" she said.

Margaret smiled graciously. "Have two," she said. "Then we'll get down to business."

Meanwhile, hidden under a bush
behind some strategically placed
branches, another top secret meeting
was taking place in the next door
garden.

"I think that's everything," said the
Leader. "I shall now put the plans
into action."

"What am I going to do?" said
Perfect Peter.

"Stand guard," said Horrid Henry.

"I always have to stand guard,"
said Peter, as the Leader crept out.

"It's not fair."

"Have you brought your spy report?" asked Margaret.

"Yes," said Susan.

"Read it aloud," said Margaret.

Susan took out a piece of paper and read:

"I watched the enemy's house for two hours yesterday morning –"

"Which morning?" interrupted Margaret.

"Saturday morning," said Susan. "A lady with grey hair and a beret walked past."

"What colour was the beret?" said Margaret.

"I don't know," said Susan.

"Call yourself a spy and you don't know what colour the beret was," said Margaret.

"Can I please continue with my report?" said Susan.

"I'm not stopping you," said Margaret.

"Then I saw the enemy leave the house with his brother and mother. The enemy kicked his brother twice. His mother shouted at him. Then I saw the postman –"

"NUNGA!" screeched a voice from outside.

Margaret and Susan froze.

"NUNGA!!!"

screeched the voice again. "I know
you're in there!"

"Aaaahh!" squeaked Susan. "It's
Henry!"

"Quick! Hide!" hissed Margaret.

The secret spies crouched behind
two boxes.

"You told him our password!"
hissed Margaret. "How dare you!"

"Wasn't me!" hissed Susan. "I
couldn't even remember it, so how
could I have told him? You told
him!"

"Didn't," hissed Margaret.

"NUNGA!!!" screeched Henry
again. "You have to let me in! I know
the password."

"What do we do?" hissed Susan.
"You said anyone who knows the
password enters."

"For the last time,

NUNGAAAAA!" shouted Horrid
Henry.

"Nunga Nu," said Margaret.
"Enter."

Henry swaggered into the tent.
Margaret glared at him.

"Don't mind if I do," said Henry,
grabbing all the chocolate biscuits and
stuffing them into his mouth. Then
he sprawled on the rug, scattering
crumbs everywhere.

"What are you doing?" said Horrid
Henry.

"Nothing," said Moody Margaret.

"Nothing," said Sour Susan.

"You are, too," said Henry.

"Mind your own business," said
Margaret. "Now, Susan, let's vote on
whether to allow boys in. I vote
No."

"I vote No, too," said Susan.

"Sorry, Henry, you can't join.
Now leave."

"No," said Henry.

"LEAVE," said Margaret.

"Make me," said Henry.

Margaret took a deep breath. Then
she opened her mouth and screamed.
No one could scream as loud, or as
long, or as piercingly, as Moody
Margaret. After a few moments,
Susan started screaming too.

Henry got to his feet, knocking
over the crate they used as a table.

"Watch out," said Henry.
"Because the Purple Hand will be
back!" He turned to go.

Moody Margaret sprang up behind
him and pushed him through the flap.
Henry landed in a heap outside.

"Can't get me!" shouted Henry.
He picked himself up and jumped
over the wall. "The Purple Hand is
the best!"

"Oh yeah," muttered Margaret.
"We'll see about that."

Henry checked over his shoulder to
make sure no one was watching.
Then he crept back to his fort.

"Smelly toads," he whispered to
the guard.

The branches parted. Henry

climbed in.

"Did you attack them?" said Peter.

"Of course," said Henry. "Didn't you hear Margaret screaming?"

"I was the one who heard their password, so I think I should have gone," said Peter.

"Whose club is this?" said Henry.

The corners of Peter's mouth began to turn down.

"Right, out!" said Henry.

"Sorry!" said Peter. "Please, Henry, can I be a real member of the Purple Hand?"

"No," said Henry. "You're too young. And don't you dare come into the fort when I'm not here."

"I won't," said Peter.

"Good," said Henry. "Now here's the plan. I'm going to set a booby trap in Margaret's tent. Then when

she goes in . . ." Henry shrieked with
laughter as he pictured Moody
Margaret covered in cold muddy
water.

All was not well back at Moody
Margaret's Secret Club.

"It's your fault," said Margaret.

"It isn't," said Susan.

"You're such a blabbermouth, and
you're a terrible spy."

"I am not," said Susan.

"Well, I'm Leader, and I ban you
from the club for a week for breaking
our sacred rule and telling the enemy
our password. Now go away."

"Oh please let me stay," said
Susan.

"No," said Margaret.

Susan knew there was no point
arguing with Margaret when she got

41

that horrible bossy look on her face.

"You're so mean," said Susan.

Moody Margaret picked up a book and started to read.

Sour Susan got up and left.

"I know what I'll do to fix Henry," thought Margaret. "I'll set a booby trap in Henry's fort. Then when he goes in . . ." Margaret shrieked with laughter as she pictured Horrid Henry covered in cold muddy water.

Just before lunch Henry sneaked into Margaret's garden holding a plastic bucket of water and some string. He stretched the string just above the ground across the entrance and suspended the bucket above, with the other end of the string tied round it.

Just after lunch Margaret sneaked into
Henry's garden holding a bucket of
water and some string. She stretched
the string across the fort's entrance
and rigged up the bucket. What she
wouldn't give to see Henry soaking
wet when he tripped over the string
and pulled the bucket of water down
on him.

Perfect Peter came into the garden carrying a ball. Henry wouldn't play with him and there was nothing to do.

Why shouldn't I go into the fort? thought Peter. I helped build it.

Next door, Sour Susan slipped into the garden. She was feeling sulky.

Why shouldn't I go into the tent? thought Susan. It's my club too.

Perfect Peter walked into the fort and tripped.

CRASH! SPLASH!

Sour Susan walked into the tent and tripped.

CRASH! SPLASH!

Horrid Henry heard howls. He ran into the garden whooping.

"Ha! Ha! Margaret! Gotcha!"

Then he stopped.

Moody Margaret heard screams. She ran into the garden cheering.

"Ha! Ha! Henry! Gotcha!"

Then she stopped.

"That's it!" shrieked Peter. "I'm leaving!"

"But it wasn't me," said Henry.

"That's it!" sobbed Susan. "I quit!"

"But it wasn't me," said Margaret.

"Rats!" said Henry.

"Rats!" said Margaret.

They glared at each other.

3

PERFECT PETER'S HORRID DAY

"Henry, use your fork!" said Dad.

"*I'm* using my fork," said Peter.

"Henry, sit down!" said Mum.

"*I'm* sitting down," said Peter.

"Henry, stop spitting!" said Dad.

"*I'm* not spitting," said Peter.

"Henry, chew with your mouth shut!" said Mum.

"*I'm* chewing with my mouth shut," said Peter.

"Henry, don't make a mess!" said Dad.

"*I'm* not making a mess," said Peter.

"What?" said Mum.

Perfect Peter was not having a perfect day.

Mum and Dad are too busy yelling at Henry all the time to notice how good *I* am, thought Peter.

When was the last time Mum and Dad had said, "Marvellous, Peter, you're using your fork!" "Wonderful, Peter, you're sitting down!" "Superb, Peter, you're not spitting!" "Fabulous, Peter, you're chewing with your mouth shut!" "Perfect, Peter, you never make a mess!"

Perfect Peter dragged himself upstairs.

Everyone just expects me to be perfect, thought Peter, as he wrote his Aunt Agnes a thank you note for the super thermal vests. It's not fair.

From downstairs came the sound

of raised voices.

"Henry, get your muddy shoes off the sofa!" yelled Dad.

"Henry, stop being so horrid!" yelled Mum.

Then Perfect Peter started to think.

What if *I* were horrid? thought Peter.

Peter's mouth dropped open. What a horrid thought! He looked around quickly, to see if anyone had noticed.

He was alone in his immaculate bedroom. No one would ever know he'd thought such a terrible thing.

But imagine being horrid. No, that would never do.

Peter finished his letter, read a few pages of his favourite magazine *Best Boy*, got into bed and turned off his light without being asked.

Imagine being horrid.

What *if* I were horrid, thought
Peter. I wonder what would happen?

When Peter woke up the next
morning, he did not dash downstairs
to get breakfast ready. Instead, he
lazed in bed for an extra five minutes.

When he finally got out of bed
Peter did not straighten the duvet.

Nor did Peter plump his pillows.

Instead Peter looked at his tidy
bedroom and had a very wicked
thought.

Quickly, before he could change
his mind, he took off his pyjama top
and did not fold it neatly. Instead he
dropped it on the floor.

Mum came in.

"Good morning, darling. You
must be tired, sleeping in."

Peter hoped Mum would notice his

untidy room.

But Mum did not say anything.

"Notice anything, Mum?" said
Peter.

Mum looked around.

"No," said Mum.

"Oh," said Peter.

"What?" said Mum.

"I haven't made my bed," said
Peter.

"Clever you to remember it's
washday," said Mum. She stripped
the sheets and duvet cover, then

51

swooped and picked up Peter's
pyjama top.

"Thank you, dear," said Mum. She
smiled and left.

Peter frowned. Clearly, he would
need to work harder at being horrid.

He looked at his beautifully
arranged books.

"No!" he gasped, as a dreadful
thought sneaked into his head.

Then Peter squared his shoulders.
Today was his horrid day, and horrid
he would be. He went up to his
books and knocked them over.

"HENRY!" bellowed Dad. "Get
up this minute!"

Henry slumped past Peter's door.

Peter decided he would call Henry
a horrid name.

"Hello, Ugly," said Peter. Then he
went wild and stuck out his tongue.

Henry marched into Peter's bedroom. He glared at Peter.

"What did you call me?" said Henry.

Peter screamed.

Mum ran into the room.

"Stop being horrid, Henry! Look what a mess you've made in here!"

"He called me Ugly," said Henry.

"Of course he didn't," said Mum.

"He did too," said Henry.

"Peter never calls people names," said Mum. "Now pick up those books you knocked over."

"I didn't knock them over," said Henry.

"Well, who did, then, the man in the moon?" said Mum.

Henry pointed at Peter.

"He did," said Henry.

"*Did* you, Peter?" asked Mum.

Peter wanted to be really really horrid and tell a lie. But he couldn't.

"I did it, Mum," said Peter. Boy, would he get told off now.

"Don't be silly, of course you didn't," said Mum. "You're just saying that to protect Henry."

Mum smiled at Peter and frowned at Henry.

"Now leave Peter alone and get dressed," said Mum.

"But it's the weekend," said Henry.

"So?" said Mum.

"But Peter's not dressed."

"I'm sure he was just about to get dressed before your barged in," said Mum. "See? He's already taken his pyjama top off."

"I don't want to get dressed," said Peter boldly.

"You poor boy," said Mum. "You must be feeling ill. Pop back into bed and I'll bring your breakfast up. Just let me put some clean sheets on."

Perfect Peter scowled a tiny scowl. Clearly, he wasn't very good at being horrid yet. He would have to try harder.

At lunch Peter ate pasta with his fingers. No one noticed.

Then Henry scooped up pasta with both fists and slurped some into his mouth.

"Henry! Use your fork!" said Dad.

Peter spat into his plate.

"Peter, are you choking?" said Dad.

Henry spat across the table.

"Henry! Stop that disgusting spitting this instant!" said Mum.

Peter chewed with his mouth open.

"Peter, is there something wrong with your teeth?" asked Mum.

Henry chomped and dribbled and gulped with his mouth as wide open as possible.

"Henry! This is your last warning. Keep your mouth shut when you eat!" shouted Dad.

Peter did not understand. Why didn't anyone notice how horrid he was? He stretched out his foot and kicked Henry under the table.

Henry kicked him back harder.

Peter shrieked.

Henry got told off. Peter got dessert.

Perfect Peter did not know what to do. No matter how hard he tried to be horrid, nothing seemed to work.

"Now boys," said Mum, "Grandma is coming for tea this afternoon. Please keep the house tidy and leave the chocolates alone."

"What chocolates?" said Henry.

"Never you mind," said Mum. "You'll have some when Grandma gets here."

Then Peter had a truly stupendously horrid idea. He left the table without waiting to be excused and sneaked into the sitting room.

Peter searched high. Peter searched low. Then Peter found a large box of chocolates hidden behind some books.

Peter opened the box. Then he took a tiny bite out of every single chocolate. When he found good ones with gooey chocolate fudge centres he ate them. The yucky raspberry and strawberry and lemon creams he put back.

Hee Hee, thought Peter. He felt excited. What he had done was absolutely awful. Mum and Dad were sure to notice.

Then Peter looked round the tidy sitting room. Why not mess it up a bit?

Peter grabbed a cushion from the sofa. He was just about to fling it on the floor when he heard someone sneaking into the room.

"What are you doing?" said Henry.

"Nothing, Ugly," said Peter.

"Don't call me Ugly, Toad," said Henry.

"Don't call me Toad, Ugly," said Peter.

"Toad!"

"Ugly!"

"TOAD!"

"UGLY!"

Mum and Dad ran in.

"Henry!" shouted Dad. "Stop being horrid!"

"I'm not being horrid!" said Henry. "Peter is calling me names."

Mum and Dad looked at each other. What was going on?

"Don't lie, Henry," said Mum.

"I did call him a name, Mum," said Peter. "I called him Ugly because he is ugly. So there."

61

Mum stared at Peter.

Dad stared at Peter.

Henry stared at Peter.

"If Peter did call you a name, it's because you called him one first," said Mum. "Now leave Peter alone."

Mum and Dad left.

"Serves you right, Henry," said Peter.

"You're very strange today," said Henry.

"No I'm not," said Peter.

"Oh yes you are," said Henry. "You can't fool me. Listen, want to play a trick on Grandma?"

"No!" said Peter.

Ding dong.

"Grandma's here!" called Dad.

Mum, Dad, Henry, Peter and Grandma sat down together in the sitting room.

"Let me take your bag, Grandma," said Henry sweetly.

"Thank you dear,' said Grandma.

When no one was looking Henry took Grandma's glasses out of her bag and hid them behind Peter's cushion.

Mum and Dad passed around tea and home-made biscuits on the best china plates.

Peter sat on the edge of the sofa and held his breath. Any second now Mum would get out the box of half-eaten chocolates.

Mum stood up and got the box.

"Peter, would you like to pass round the chocolates?" said Mum.

"Okay," said Peter. His knees felt wobbly. Everyone was about to find out what a horrid thing he had done.

Peter held out the box.

"Would you like a chocolate, Mum?" said Peter. His heart pounded.

"No thanks," said Mum.

"What about me?" said Henry.

"Would you like a chocolate, Dad?" said Peter. His hands shook.

"No thanks," said Dad.

"What about me!" said Henry.

"Shh, Henry," said Mum. "Don't be so rude."

"Would you like a chocolate, Grandma?" said Peter.

There was no escape now. Grandma loved chocolates.

"Yes, please!" said Grandma. She peered closely into the box. "Let me see, what shall I choose? Now, where are my specs?"

Grandma reached into her bag and fumbled about.

"That's funny," said Grandma. "I was sure I'd brought them. Never mind."

Grandma reached into the box, chose a chocolate and popped it into her mouth.

"Oh," said Grandma. "Strawberry cream. Go on, Peter, have a chocolate."

"No thanks," said Peter.

"WHAT ABOUT ME!" screamed Horrid Henry.

"None for you," said Dad. "That's not how you ask."

Peter gritted his teeth. If no one was going to notice the chewed chocolates he'd have to do it himself.

"I will have a chocolate," announced Peter loudly. "Hey! Who's eaten all the fudge ones? And who's taken bites out of the rest?"

"Henry!" yelled Mum. "I've told you a million times to leave the chocolates alone!"

"It wasn't me!" said Henry. "It was Peter!"

"Stop blaming Peter,' said Dad. "You know he never eats sweets."

"It's not fair!" shrieked Henry. Then he snatched the box from Peter. "I want some CHOCOLATES!"

Peter snatched it back. The open box fell to the floor. Chocolates flew everywhere.

"HENRY, GO TO YOUR ROOM!" yelled Mum.

"IT'S NOT FAIR!" screeched Henry. "I'll get you for this, Peter!"

Then Horrid Henry ran out of the room, slamming the door behind him.

Grandma patted the sofa beside her. Peter sat down. He could not believe it. What did a boy have to do to get noticed?

"How's my best boy?" asked Grandma.

Peter sighed.

Grandma gave him a big hug. "You're the best boy in the world, Peter, did you know that?"

Peter glowed. Grandma was right! He was the best.

But wait. Today he was horrid.

NO! He was perfect. His horrid

day was over.

He was much happier being perfect, anyway. Being horrid was horrible.

I've had my horrid day, thought Peter. Now I can be perfect again.

What a marvellous idea. Peter smiled and leaned back against the cushion.

CRUNCH!

"Oh dear," said Grandma. "That sounds like my specs. I wonder how they got there."

Mum looked at Peter.

Dad looked at Peter.

"It wasn't me!" said Peter.

"Of course not," said Grandma. "I must have dropped them. Silly me."

"Hmmmn," said Dad.

Perfect Peter ran into the kitchen and looked about. Now that I'm perfect again, what good deeds can I do? he thought.

Then Peter noticed all the dirty tea cups and plates piled up on the worktop. He had never done the washing up all by himself before. Mum and Dad would be so pleased.

Peter carefully washed and dried all the dishes.

Then he stacked them up and carried them to the cupboard.

"BOOOOOOO!" shrieked Horrid Henry, leaping out from behind the door.

CRASH!

Henry vanished.

Mum and Dad ran in.

The best china lay in pieces all over the floor.

"PETER!!!" yelled Mum and Dad.

"YOU HORRID BOY!" yelled Mum.

"GO TO YOUR ROOM!" yelled Dad.

"But . . . but . . ." gasped Peter.

"NO BUTS!" shouted Mum. "GO! Oh, my lovely dishes!"

Perfect Peter ran to his room.

"AHHHHHHHHHHHH!" shrieked Peter.

4

HORRID HENRY'S BIRTHDAY PARTY

February was Horrid Henry's favourite month.

His birthday was in February.

"It's my birthday soon!" said Henry every day after Christmas. "And my birthday party! Hurray!"

February was Horrid Henry's parents' least favourite month.

"It's Henry's birthday soon," said Dad, groaning.

"And his birthday party," said Mum, groaning even louder.

Every year they thought Henry's

birthday parties could not get worse. But they always did.

Every year Henry's parents said they would never ever let Henry have a birthday party again. But every year they gave Henry one absolutely last final chance.

Henry had big plans for this year's party.

"I want to go to Lazer Zap," said Henry. He'd been to Lazer Zap for Tough Toby's party. They'd had a great time dressing up as spacemen and blasting each other in dark tunnels all afternoon.

"NO!" said Mum. "Too violent."

"I agree," said Dad.

"And too expensive," said Mum.

"I agree," said Dad.

There was a moment's silence.

"However," said Dad, "it does

73

mean the party wouldn't be here."

Mum looked at Dad. Dad looked at Mum.

"How do I book?" said Mum.

"Hurray!" shrieked Henry. "Zap! Zap! Zap!"

Horrid Henry sat in his fort holding a pad of paper. On the front cover in big capital letters Henry wrote:

HENRY'S PARTY PLANS.

TOP SECRET!!!!

At the top of the first page Henry had written:

GUESTS

A long list followed. Then Henry stared at the names and chewed his pencil.

Actually, I don't want Margaret, thought Henry. Too moody.

He crossed out Moody Margaret's

name.

And I definitely don't want Susan.
Too crabby.

In fact, I don't want any girls at all,
thought Henry. He crossed out
Clever Clare and Lazy Linda.

Then there was Anxious Andrew.

Nope, thought Henry, crossing
him off. He's no fun.

Toby was possible, but Henry
didn't really like him.

Out went Tough Toby.

William?

No way, thought Henry. He'll be
crying the second he gets zapped.

Out went Weepy William.

Ralph?

Henry considered. Ralph would be
good because he was sure to get into
trouble. On the other hand, he hadn't
invited Henry to *his* party.

Rude Ralph was struck off.

So were Babbling Bob, Jolly Josh, Greedy Graham and Dizzy Dave. And absolutely no way was Peter coming anywhere near him on his birthday.

Ahh, that was better. No horrid kids would be coming to *his* party.

There was only one problem. Every single name was crossed off.

No guests meant no presents.

Henry looked at his list. Margaret was a moody old grouch and he hated her, but she did sometimes give good gifts. He still had the jumbo box of day-glo slime she'd given him last year.

And Toby *had* invited Henry to *his* party.

And Dave was always spinning round like a top, falling and knocking

things over which was fun. Graham
would eat too much and burp. And
Ralph was sure to say rude words and
make all the grown-ups angry.

Oh, let them all come, thought
Henry. Except Peter, of course. The
more guests I have, the more presents
I get!

Henry turned to the next page and wrote:

PRESENTS I WANT
Super Soaker 2000, the best water
blaster ever
Spy Fax
Micro Machines
Slime
GameBoy
Inter-galactic Samurai Gorillas
Stink bombs
Pet rats
Whoopee cushion
25-gear mountain bike
Money

He'd leave the list lying around where Mum and Dad were sure to find it.

"I've done the menu for the party,"

said Mum. "What do you think?"

MUM'S MENU
carrot sticks
cucumber sandwiches
peanut butter sandwiches
grapes
raisins
apple juice
carrot cake

'Blecccccch," said Henry. "I don't want that horrible food at my party. I want food that I like."

HENRY'S MENU
Pickled Onion Monster Munch
Smoky Spider Shreddies
Super Spicy Hedgehog Crisps
Crunchy Crackles
Twizzle Fizzle Sticks
Purple Planet-buster Drink

chocolate bars
chocolate eggs
Chocolate Monster Cake

"You can't just have junk food,"
said Mum.

"It's not junk food," said Henry.
"Crisps are made from potatoes, and
Monster Munch has onions – that's
two vegetables."

"Henry . . ." said Mum. She
looked fierce.

Henry looked at his menu. Then he
added, in small letters at the bottom:

peanut butter sandwiches

"But only in the middle of the
table," said Henry. "So no one has to
eat them who doesn't want them."

"All right," said Mum. Years of

fighting with Henry about his parties
had worn her down.

"And Peter's not coming," said
Henry.

"What?!" said Perfect Peter,
looking up from polishing his shoes.

"Peter is your brother. Of course
he's invited."

Henry scowled.

"But he'll ruin everything."

"No Peter, no party," said Mum.

Henry pretended he was a fire-
breathing dragon.

"Owww!" shrieked Peter.

"Don't be horrid, Henry!" yelled Mum.

"All right," said Henry. "He can come. But you'd better keep out of my way," he hissed at Peter.

"Mum!" wailed Peter. "Henry's being mean to me."

"Stop it, Henry," said Mum.

Henry decided to change the subject fast.

"What about party bags?" said Henry. "I want everyone to have Slime, and loads and loads and loads of sweets! Dirt Balls, Nose Pickers and Foam Teeth are the best."

"We'll see," said Mum. She looked at the calendar. Only two more days. Soon it would be over.

Henry's birthday arrived at last.

"Happy birthday, Henry!" said Mum.

"Happy birthday, Henry!" said Dad.

"Happy birthday, Henry!" said Peter.

"Where are my presents?" said Henry.

Dad pointed. Horrid Henry attacked the pile.

Mum and Dad had given him a *First Encyclopedia*, Scrabble, a fountain pen, a hand-knitted cardigan, a globe, and three sets of vests and pants.

"Oh," said Henry. He pushed the dreadful presents aside.

"Anything else?" he asked hopefully. Maybe they were keeping the super soaker for last.

"I've got a present for you," said Peter. "I chose it myself."

Henry tore off the wrapping paper.
It was a tapestry kit.

"Yuck!" said Henry.

"I'll have it if you don't want it,"
said Peter.

"No!" said Henry, snatching up
the kit.

"Wasn't it a great idea to have
Henry's party at Lazer Zap?" said
Dad.

84

"Yes," said Mum. "No mess, no fuss."

They smiled at each other.

Ring ring.

Dad answered the phone. It was the Lazer Zap lady.

"Hello! I was just ringing to check the birthday boy's name," she said. "We like to announce it over our loudspeaker during the party."

Dad gave Henry's name.

A terrible scream came from the other end of the phone. Dad held the receiver away from his ear.

The shrieking and screaming continued.

'Hmmmn," said Dad. "I see. Thank you."

Dad hung up. He looked pale.

"Henry!"

"Yeah?"

"Is it true that you wrecked the place when you went to Lazer Zap with Toby?" said Dad.

"No!" said Henry. He tried to look harmless.

"And trampled on several children?"

"No!" said Henry.

"Yes you did," said Perfect Peter. "And what about all the lasers you broke?"

"What lasers?" said Henry.

"And the slime you put in the space suits?" said Peter.

"That wasn't me, telltale," shrieked Henry. "What about my party?"

"I'm afraid Lazer Zap have banned you," said Dad.

"But what about Henry's party?" said Mum. She looked pale.

86

"But what about my party?!"
wailed Henry. "I want to go to Lazer
Zap!"

"Never mind," said Dad brightly.
"I know lots of good games."

Ding dong.

It was the first guest, Sour Susan.
She held a large present.

Henry snatched the package.

It was a pad of paper and some felt
tip pens.

"How lovely," said Mum. "What do you say, Henry?"

"I've already got that," said Henry.

"Henry!" said Mum. "Don't be horrid!"

I don't care, thought Henry. This was the worst day of his life.

Ding dong.

It was the second guest, Anxious Andrew. He held a tiny present.

Henry snatched the package.

"It's awfully small," said Henry, tearing off the wrapping. "And it smells."

It was a box of animal soaps.

"How super," said Dad. "What do you say, Henry?"

"Ugghhh!" said Henry.

"Henry!" said Dad. "Don't be horrid."

Henry stuck out his lower lip.

"It's my party and I'll do what I want," muttered Henry.

"Watch your step, young man," said Dad.

Henry stuck out his tongue behind Dad's back.

More guests arrived.

Lazy Linda gave him a "Read and Listen Cassette of favourite fairy tales: Cinderella, Snow White, and Sleeping Beauty."

"Fabulous," said Mum.

"Yuck!" said Henry.

Clever Clare handed him a square package.

Henry held it by the corners.

"It's a book," he groaned.

"My favourite present!" said Peter.

"Wonderful," said Mum. "What is it?"

Henry unwrapped it slowly.

"*Cook Your Own Healthy Nutritious Food.*"

"Great!" said Perfect Peter. "Can I borrow it?"

"NO!" screamed Henry. Then he threw the book on the floor and stomped on it.

"Henry!" hissed Mum. "I'm warning you. When someone gives you a present you say thank you."

Rude Ralph was the last to arrive.

He handed Henry a long rectangular package wrapped in newspaper.

It was a Super Soaker 2000 water blaster.

"Oh," said Mum.

"Put it away," said Dad.

"Thank you Ralph," beamed Henry. "Just what I wanted."

"Let's start with Pass the Parcel," said Dad.

"I hate Pass the Parcel," said Horrid Henry. What a horrible party this was.

"I love Pass the Parcel," said Perfect Peter.

"I don't want to play," said Sour Susan.

"When do we eat?" said Greedy Graham.

Dad started the music.

"Pass the parcel, William," said Dad.

"No!" shrieked William. "It's mine!"

"But the music is still playing," said Dad.

William burst into tears.

Horrid Henry tried to snatch the parcel.

Dad stopped the music.

William stopped crying instantly and tore off the wrapping.

"A granola bar," he said.

"That's a terrible prize," said Rude Ralph.

"Is it my turn yet?" said Anxious Andrew.

"When do we eat?" said Greedy Graham.

"I hate Pass the Parcel," screamed

Henry. "I want to play something else."

"Musical Statues!" announced Mum brightly.

"You're out, Henry," said Dad. "You moved."

"I didn't," said Henry.

"Yes you did," said Toby.

"No I didn't," said Henry. "I'm not leaving."

"That's not fair," shrieked Sour Susan.

"I'm not playing," whined Dizzy Dave.

"I'm tired," sulked Lazy Linda.

"I hate Musical Statues," moaned Moody Margaret.

"Where's my prize?" demanded Rude Ralph.

"A book mark?" said Ralph.

"That's it?"

"Tea time!" said Dad.

The children pushed and shoved their way to the table, grabbing and snatching at the food.

"I hate fizzy drinks," said Tough Toby.

"I feel sick," said Greedy Graham.

"Where are the carrot sticks?" said Perfect Peter.

Horrid Henry sat at the head of the table.

He didn't feel like throwing food at Clare.

He didn't feel like rampaging with Toby and Ralph.

He didn't even feel like kicking Peter.

He wanted to be at Lazer Zap.

Then Henry had a wonderful,

spectacular idea. He got up and
sneaked out of the room.

"Party bags," said Dad.

"What's in them?" said Tough
Toby.

"Seedlings," said Mum.

"Where are the sweets?" said
Greedy Graham.

"This is the worst party bag I've
ever had," said Rude Ralph.

There was a noise outside.

Then Henry burst into the kitchen,
supersoaker in hand.

"ZAP! ZAP! ZAP!" shrieked Henry, drenching everyone with water. "Ha! Ha! Gotcha!"

Splat went the cake.

Splash went the drinks.

"EEEEEEEEEEEEEKKK!" shrieked the sopping wet children.

"HENRY!!!!!" yelled Mum and Dad.

"YOU HORRID BOY!" yelled Mum. Water dripped from her hair. "GO TO YOUR ROOM!"

"THIS IS YOUR LAST PARTY EVER!" yelled Dad. Water dripped from his clothes.

But Henry didn't care. They said that every year.